WELCOME TO RUMOURVILLE

BEWARE THE BLUE BAGOO!

Brimming with creative inspiration, how-to projects, and useful information to enrich your everyday life, quarto.com is a favorite destination for those pursuing their interests and passions.

Inspiring | Educating | Creating | Entertaining

First published in 2023 by Happy Yak,
an imprint of The Quarto Group.
The Old Brewery, 6 Blundell Street,
London N7 9BH, United Kingdom.
T (0)20 7700 6700 F (0)20 7700 8066
www.quarto.com

A catalogue record for this book is available from the British Library.

ISBN: 978-0-7112-6782-4
eISBN: 978-0-7112-6785-5

9 8 7 6 5 4 3 2 1

Manufactured in Guangdong, China TT112022

FSC MIX Paper from responsible sources FSC® C016973

For Colin West and Cathy MacLennan – thank you for all of the support, encouragement and incredible kindness you have gifted me! – K.N.

This book is for you, my Blue Bagoo! – A.S.

KARL NEWSON

ANDREA STEGMAIER

BEWARE THE BLUE BAGOO!

A Blue Bagoo?
A Blue *Bagoo*?!
Who-oh-who
is the Blue Bagoo?

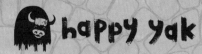
happy yak

The **Blue Bagoo** is as tall as a tree.

It lives in a cave.

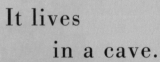

It swims in the sea.

It's covered in fur!

It's spiky...

and blue.

BEWARE THE BLUE BAGOO!

My grandma was made
into Blue Bagoo stew.

My parrot was squashed
by a Blue Bagoo shoe.

My hat disappeared without a clue!

BEWARE
THE
BLUE
BAGOO!

CHOMP! CHOMP!

CHOMP! CHOMP!

To make a meal of
YOU!

The Blue Bagoo is as bad as they come.

It nibbled my dad.

It gobbled my mum!

It's hungry for lunch and it's coming for **YOU!**

But who *is*
the **Blue Bagoo?**

I am the
Blue Bagoo!

You're NOT very grizzly...
You're NOT very mean.
You're FAR from the worst
thing that I've ever seen!

You're nowhere *near* wild...
You're as cute as can be!

(And not *half* as tall as a tree!)

There's been a mistake!
You've got it all wrong.
You need a new sign...
You need a new song!

A rumour has spread
and it's very unfair.

There's really no need to be—

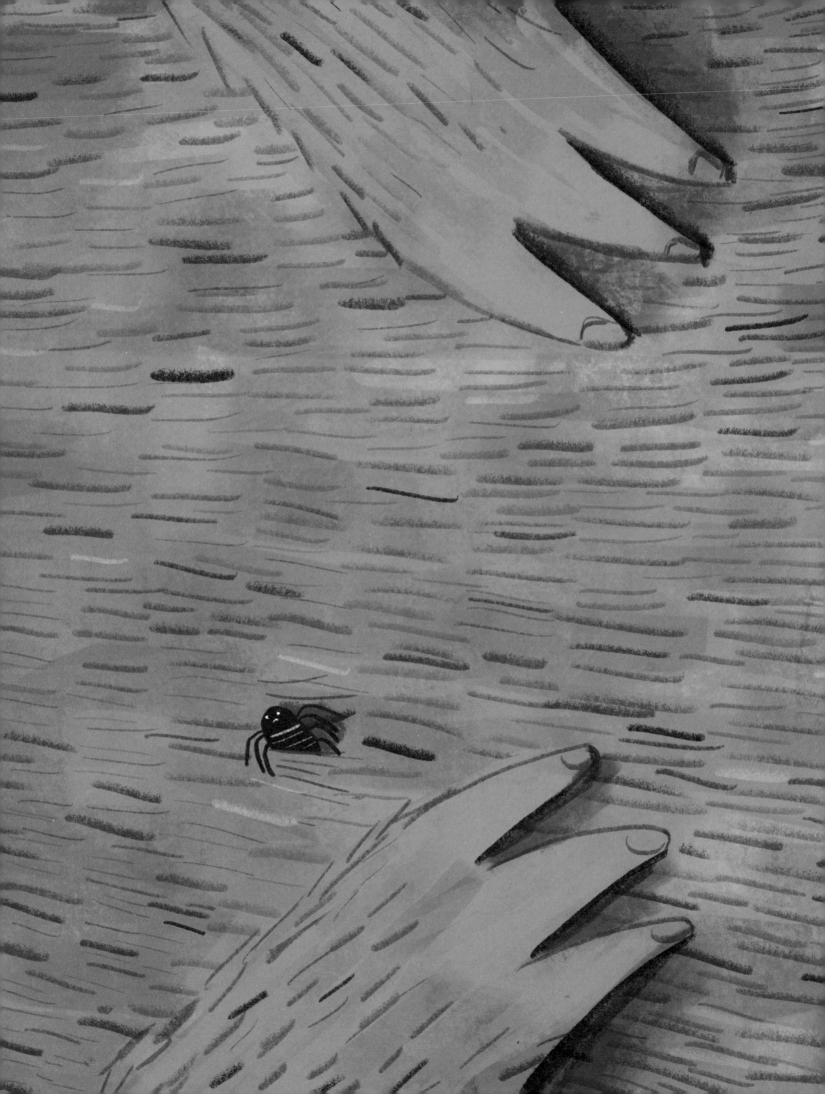

WHERE ARE YOU ALL GOING?

Oh dear... it's YOU!
THE BLUE BAGOO!

How silly of me...

The rumours ARE true!

You've eaten them all...

And now you'll eat me!

No! This is the
Blue Bagee!

The Blue Bagee is as kind as they come...

She'll never creep up with a

dum-

dum-

DUUUM!

She only eats cake!

There are more of us, too...

WE'RE SORRY, BLUE BAGOO!

Isn't it strange, how a rumour can *grow*
out of fear for a thing that we don't really know?

And a word that's misheard can become such a *BEAST*?!
We got it put right in the end, at least.

MYSTERY SOLVED –
it was all a mistake...
and sometimes mistakes are so *easy* to make.

But I think if we're *friendly*, and *caring*, and *kind*,
and it's *love* that we give...

... it is *love* that we'll find.

THE END